COMMUNITY CONNECTIONS

WHAT SHOULD I DO?

IN THE CAR

BY WIL MARA

CHERRY LAKE Publishing

Published in the United States of America by Cherry Lake Publishing
Ann Arbor, Michigan
www.cherrylakepublishing.com

Content Adviser: Karen Sheehan, MD, MPH, Children's Memorial Hospital, Chicago, Illinois

Photo Credits: Cover ©iStockphoto.com/kate_sept2004; page 5, ©Media Bakery; page 7, ©egd/Shutterstock, Inc.; page 9, ©Andrr/Shutterstock, Inc.; page 11, ©Anna Baburkina/Dreamstime.com; page 13, ©Pam Mamsch; page 15, ©Marcel Jancovic/Shutterstock, Inc.; page 17, ©Bendao/Dreamstime.com; page 19, ©Picture Partners/Alamy; page 21, ©Monkey Business Images/Shutterstock, Inc.

LIBRARY OF CONGRESS CATALOGING-IN-PUBLICATION DATA
Mara, Wil.
What should I do? In the car/by Wil Mara.
p. cm.—(Community connections)
Includes bibliographical references and index.
ISBN-13: 978-1-61080-052-5 (lib. bdg.)
ISBN-10: 1-61080-052-4 (lib. bdg.)
1. Child restraint systems in automobiles—Juvenile literature. 2. Automobiles—Safety measures—Juvenile literature. I. Title. II. Series.
HE5620.S34M37 2011
613.6'8—dc22 2010053593

Cherry Lake Publishing would like to acknowledge the work of The Partnership for 21st Century Skills. Please visit *www.21stcenturyskills.org* for more information.

Printed in the United States of America
Corporate Graphics Inc.
July 2011
CLFA09

IN THE CAR

CONTENTS

WHAT SHOULD I DO?

SAFETY FIRST

Riding in a car can be **dangerous**. Sometimes cars get into **accidents**. You could get hurt if you were in a car accident.

There are some rules you can follow to keep safe. Do you know what they are?

If you follow the rules, you can stay safe in your car.

LOOK!

Look out the window the next time you are riding in a car. Are the children in other cars sitting down? Are they being safe? Are they making it harder for their parents to pay attention to the road?

MANY THINGS CAN HAPPEN

You might think you are safe inside a car. Cars are heavy and made of strong metal. It is like having a shell around you. But sometimes that is not enough.

A car can hit something. It can also be hit *by* something. Even strong metal can be smashed.

Cars are strong, but they can still be damaged in an accident.

Wet or icy roads can make it hard for drivers to control their cars. Someone might walk in front of a car. Then the driver would have to stop the car very quickly.

The driver of another car could lose control and hit the car that you are in. Accidents like this happen every day.

Drivers must be extra careful when driving on snowy streets.

MAKE A GUESS!

Look around each time you get into the car. Will it be safe to drive? Is it raining or snowing? Do your parents seem too tired to drive well? Do not be afraid to say something if you feel unsafe.

SMART SAFETY RULES

Always wear a **seat belt**. It will hold you in your seat if the car gets into an accident.

Use a **booster seat** if you are less than 57 inches (145 centimeters) tall. Booster seats make the seat belt fit over you much better.

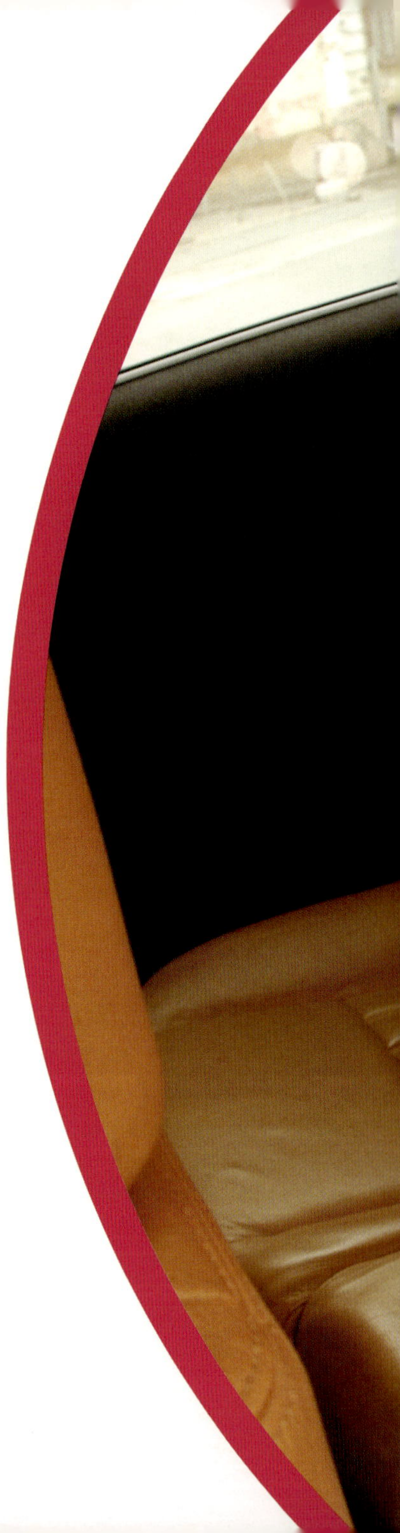

Booster seats help make sure that your seat belt will protect you if there is an accident.

It is dangerous to **distract** the person who is driving. You might distract the driver if you make loud noises or throw things. Playing with the buttons that open the doors and windows can also distract the driver.

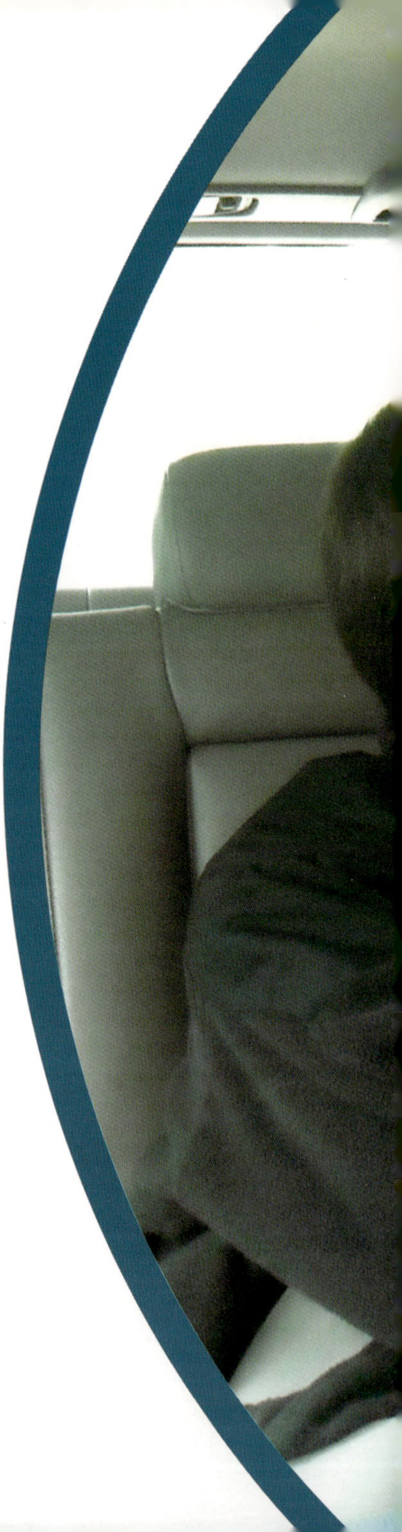

Fooling around in the car can distract the driver.

CREATE!

Create a car safety game with your parents. You can get points for following the safety rules. But you will lose points if you forget the rules. Your brothers and sisters can play, too.

Do you have a baby sister or brother? Babies should always ride in **infant seats**. These seats should face the back of the car. That means your sister or brother will face the back window. It might look funny, but it helps keep a baby safe if there is an accident.

Infant seats help keep babies safe in cars.

Toddler seats are for small children who are no longer babies. Do you have a younger brother or sister who uses a toddler seat? Ask your parents to show you how the seat is attached. Toddler seats are unsafe if they are not attached correctly. Don't try to take the seat out of the car or move it.

Toddler seats let small children face the front of the car.

OTHER RULES TO REMEMBER

You should always sit in the backseat of a car. It is not safe for children to sit in the front seat.

Make sure there are no loose things lying around. They can bounce around and hurt you if the car crashes. Also, make sure you are not left alone in a car.

Children should always sit in the backseat of a car.

Do not play in or near cars that are running. Even parked cars that are running can be dangerous.

Don't play with car locks. You could lock yourself inside. And stay out of the trunk! You could also get locked in there.

Cars take you and your family to many places. If you follow the rules, you can stay safe and have fun!

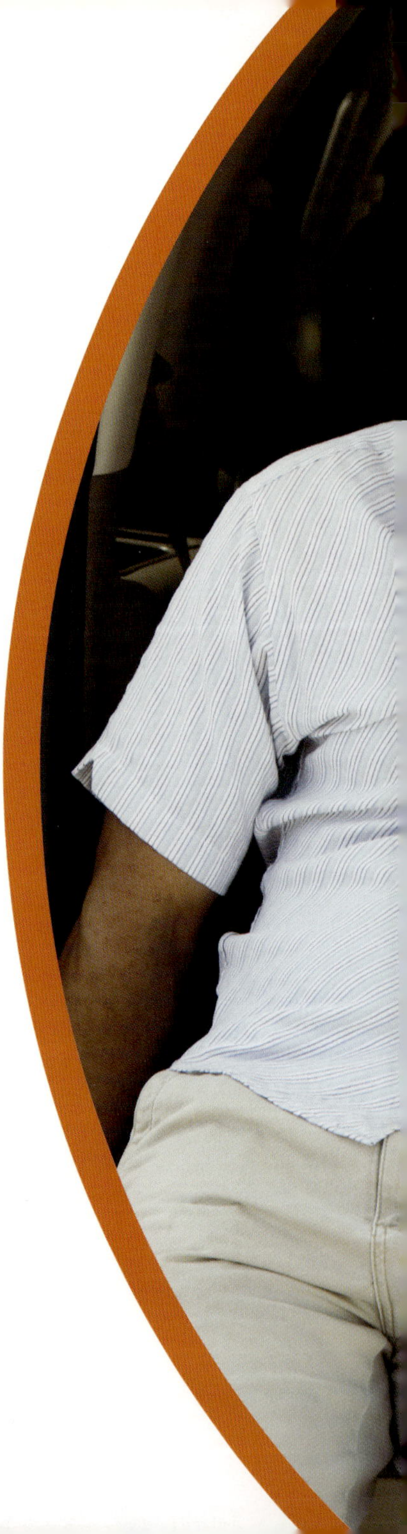

How will you help your family stay safe in the car?

THINK!

Think about all the rules you need to follow each time you get into the car. Make a list and keep it in the car. Check the list each time you get in. You can be in charge of car safety for your family!

GLOSSARY

accidents (AK-si-duhnts) when a car hits something

booster seat (BOO-stur SEET) a padded car seat that makes children taller so seat belts will fit the right way

dangerous (DANE-jur-us) potentially harmful

distract (dis-TRAKT) to keep from paying attention

infant seats (IN-fuhnt SEETS) padded, cradle-shaped car seats for babies

seat belt (SEET BELT) a strap that holds you in your seat

toddler seats (TODD-lur SEETS) padded car seats made for a young child who has become too big for an infant seat

FIND OUT MORE

BOOKS

Barraclough, Sue. *Road Safety.* Chicago: Heinemann Library, 2008.

Llewellyn, Claire. *On the Road.* Hauppauge, NY: Barron's Educational Series, 2006.

Mattern, Joanne. *Staying Safe in the Car.* Milwaukee: Weekly Reader Early Learning Library, 2007.

WEB SITES

KidsHealth—Staying Safe in the Car and on the Bus
kidshealth.org/kid/watch/out/car_safety.html
Check out some tips for wearing seat belts the right way and staying safe on your school bus.

National Highway Traffic Safety Administration—Child Safety
www.nhtsa.gov/Safety/CPS
Find out which kinds of safety seats are right for you and your family members.

INDEX

ABOUT THE AUTHOR

Wil Mara is the award-winning author of more than 120 books, many of which are educational titles for children. More information about his work can be found at *www.wilmara.com.*